It's a Baby,
Andy Russell

Andy Russell's other (mis)adventures:

**The Many Troubles
of Andy Russell**

Andy and Tamika

**School Trouble
for Andy Russell**

**Parachuting Hamsters
and Andy Russell**

**Andy Russell,
NOT Wanted by the Police**

It's a Baby,
Andy
Russell

David A. Adler

With illustrations by
Leanne Franson

Gulliver Books • Harcourt, Inc.

Orlando   Austin   New York   San Diego   Toronto   London

www.HarcourtBooks.com

Gulliver Books is a trademark of Harcourt, Inc., registered in
the United States of America and/or other jurisdictions.

Library of Congress Cataloging-in-Publication Data
Adler, David A.
It's a baby, Andy Russell/by David A. Adler; with illustrations
by Leanne Franson.
p. cm.
Summary: While Andy's parents are at the hospital with a new baby,
leaving Andy and his sister at home with their germaphobic aunt,
Andy thinks that Aunt Janet wants him to get rid of his pets.
[1. Aunts—Fiction. 2. Cleanliness—Fiction. 3. Family life—Fiction.]
I. Title: It's a baby, Andy Russell. II. Franson, Leanne, ill. III. Title.
PZ7.A2615It 2005
[Fic]—dc22 2004014997
. ISBN 0-15-216742-0

Text set in Century Old Style
Designed by Suzanne Fridley

First edition

A C E G H F D B

Printed in the United States of America

To my nephew Matthew

Contents

It's a Baby,
Andy
Russell

Chapter 1
You Have Six Messages

Yikes!" Rachel Russell hollered. She turned and called to Andy, "You're in trouble now. Real trouble. Just wait till Mom sees this mess."

Andy Russell, his sister, Rachel, and their friend Tamika Anderson had just come home from school. Rachel was standing by the open front door to the house.

"Let me see," Andy said. He hurried up the front walk to the house and looked in.

The closet door was open. Coats, hats, scarves,

1

gloves, umbrellas, and the morning newspaper were on the floor.

"I'm not in trouble. I didn't make this mess and you know it," Andy said. "I was in school all day. We got on and off the bus together."

"Then who did?" Rachel asked.

How would I know? Andy thought, but that's not what he said. Instead he joked, "Who did? It was my teacher, Ms. Roman. She found out I was the one who spilled the doughnut holes all over her desk and she's getting even."

"Spilled doughnut holes on her desk," Tamika said. "That's funny."

Andy bowed.

"Well, this mess isn't funny," Rachel said. "Maybe a raccoon came down the chimney. I've heard they do that."

Rachel and Tamika cautiously walked in. They quietly put their book bags down, stood by the front door, and looked around.

Andy wasn't cautious at all. He walked right past them to the kitchen.

"Hey," he called. "Look in here."

The breakfast dishes were still on the table.

The milk and juice containers were out. Mr. and Mrs. Russell's cups still had coffee in them.

"Mom and Dad rushed off," Rachel said. "Maybe Mom is having the baby and that's why the house is a mess."

"The baby!" Andy shouted. "My brother was born! My brother, Evan, was born!" He threw the newspaper into the air. "Two Russell boys and one Russell girl." He pointed to Rachel and laughed. "You're the odd one. It's a boys' house now."

"Maybe," Rachel said, "and maybe not. Maybe the baby is a girl."

"No it's not. I mean no *he's* not. The doctor said it's a boy. Mom took that test."

"The test might be wrong," Rachel explained. "We'll have to wait until the baby is born to be sure. She might be a girl. Then you'll be the odd one. You're the odd one, anyway."

"I am not odd. I'm just exuberant. Dad said so."

Tamika interrupted them. "Let's look for a note. Your parents must have left a note."

"There's nothing on the counter," Andy said.

"And nothing on the refrigerator," Tamika added.

"They were probably in too much of a rush to

write a note," Rachel said. "But maybe they called from the hospital and left a message." She pushed the PLAY button on the answering machine.

Hello, the machine said. *You have six messages.* Then the tape began to rewind.

"This is your first message," Andy announced. Then he said "Hello" in a pretend baby's voice. "This is your new brother talking. GET ME OUT OF HERE. GET ME OUT OF THIS HOSPITAL!"

"You think a baby can talk," Rachel said. "You probably think the baby will go to school with us and help you with your homework."

"Sure he will. We Russell guys are pretty smart."
Message one.

"Hello? Hello? Are you there, Anne? This is Jacob Kamen. Are you in the hospital? If I don't hear from you soon I'll get a substitute for your classes."

Mrs. Russell was a high school math teacher.
Message two.

"Charles? Charles? This is Bob. Where are you? Please, call and tell me what's going on."

"He's Dad's boss," Rachel told Tamika. Mr. Russell was a carpenter.
Message three.

"Carol? Carol? This is Jake. I know you're there. Please, pick up the telephone."

"There's no Carol here," Andy told the answering machine. "You have the wrong number."

Jake said, "Come on, Carol."

"Didn't you hear me?" Andy asked. "There's no Carol here."

"Poor Jake," Tamika sighed.

"And poor Carol," Rachel added. "I bet she's waiting for his call."

"I'm sorry you feel like that," Jake said. "Please, call me if you want to talk."

Message four.

"Hello. Rachel, Andy, and Tamika. This is Dad. I'm at the hospital. *We're* at the hospital. We didn't tell you, but last night, Mom felt contractions. And this morning, just after you left for school, they were more intense. The baby is coming. I'm so excited. *We're* so excited."

"Yes!" Rachel, Andy, and Tamika shouted.

"We don't know when, but soon," Mr. Russell continued. "Real soon. Mom is OK. But I'm not sure I am. I can't keep still. I have a whole bunch of calls to make now, to Mom's principal, Mr.

Kamen, and to my boss, Bob, and Aunt Janet. She'll come to help out while Mom is in the hospital. I have to hurry back to Mom. And I have to make those calls. And I have to . . . I should make a list of everything I have to do. Bye."

"Yes, make a list," Rachel told the answering machine.

"And go back to Mrs. Russell. She needs you," Tamika said.

"BUT *DON'T* CALL AUNT JANET!" Andy hollered.

"Why not? What's so bad about Aunt Janet?" Tamika asked.

Message five.

"Hi. This is Betty. Mr. Kamen just told me why you're not here. I'm so excited. Good luck."

"Aunt Janet is a worrier and a complainer," Andy said.

"Andy's right," Rachel agreed. "Whenever we do something, she complains we did it wrong."

Message six.

"Hello. This is Aunt Janet."

"No," Andy groaned and put his hands over his ears. "I'm not listening."

"It's ten minutes after three. Doesn't your school end at three? Wait, I think it's ten after three, or maybe it's ten after four. Maybe I forgot to move my watch back when I left the house. I wish we lived in the same time zone. Oh my! It's ten after four and you're still not home! Now I'm worried."

Rachel leaned forward. "No. It was ten after three when you called," she told the answering machine. "And we don't live next door to the school. We take the bus home and that takes time."

Andy had taken his hands away from his ears. He got even closer to the machine. "Did you ever hear of a bus?" he asked.

"I'll be at your house in half an hour," Aunt Janet said. "We have to get the house ready for the baby."

That was your last message.

"Did you hear that?" Rachel asked. "We got her worried because she didn't know the time. Suddenly it's our fault."

Andy said, "Once, she was here when Mom and Dad went on a vacation. I made my bed and she got all upset. 'With the bed made,' she said, 'I don't know if you made it this morning or if it's

8

still made from yesterday because you didn't go to sleep last night. Now I'm so worried. Children need their sleep.'"

"That's strange," Tamika said. "*You* made your bed!"

"That's what I mean. I did something good and Aunt Janet was worried."

"She always worries," Rachel said. "The last time she was here, I was thinking about a history test I was having, so I ate my breakfast real slow. Aunt Janet thought I was sick and took my temperature."

"I saw that, so I ate fast," Andy added, "and she got all worried that I would choke."

"And when she worries she gets her beagle look," Rachel said. "Her eyebrows go up and her lips curl down."

"Yeah," Andy said. "THE BEAGLE!"

He raised his eyebrows and pouted.

Rachel said, "When she takes care of us, whatever we do is not good enough. When we wash the dishes, they're not clean enough. When we straighten our rooms, they're not neat enough."

"She'll be here soon," Tamika warned. "Let's

clean up before your Aunt Janet sees this mess and complains."

I will erase your messages.

"Yeah," Andy said to the answering machine. "And be sure to erase the one from Aunt Janet."

Chapter 2
It's Aunt Janet

Rachel emptied the coffee cups and washed them. Andy put away the milk and juice containers. He carried the dirty dishes to the sink.

"You must be exaggerating about your aunt," Tamika said.

"Exaggerating!" Andy cried and waved a dirty dish. "She's a worrier, a complainer, and I forgot to tell you something else she is. She's bossy. She's got a sign in the bathroom of her apartment that

11

says, 'Flush and check. If you must, flush again.' Now that's bossy *and* gross."

Rachel dialed the telephone. "You've got to hear this," she told Tamika. Rachel pressed the speaker button.

This is Janet Russell. I'm a nurse. If this is a medical emergency you should call a doctor or a hospital. And I hope you feel better. Oh, and if you want to leave a message, wait for the beep. Then be brief and speak clearly and please don't mumble. Bye.

"Call a doctor! Don't mumble!" Rachel said. "See how bossy she is?"

"Well," Andy announced, "I'm leaving a message." He grabbed the telephone.

Beep.

"Mumble, mumble, mumble, mumble," Andy said in a squeaky voice. Then he squeaked louder. "MUMBLE, MUMBLE, MUMBLE, MUMBLE, MUMBLE, MUMBLE."

He gave the receiver to Rachel. "I don't want it," she said and quickly hung up.

"Ha!" Andy said. "I mumbled to Aunt Janet."

"So what," Rachel said. "You disguised your voice. She won't even know it's you."

Andy looked at the telephone. Then he looked at Rachel and laughed.

"What?" Rachel asked. "What's so funny?"

"I disguised *my* voice, but you didn't disguise *yours.* When Aunt Janet hears you say 'I don't want it' just before you hung up the phone, she'll think you're the mumbler."

"Me!" Rachel cried and clenched her fists. "She'd better not think it's me. If she blames me, I'll tell her it was you."

"Well, I agree with Aunt Janet," Tamika said. "People shouldn't mumble when they leave a message."

"You agree with Aunt Janet?" Andy asked.

"Yes. Listen to this. 'Wabling fasince to arrow. The Sandy.' Some gravelly voice person once mumbled that message into my answering machine. It was scary."

"I don't mumble," Andy protested, "and I didn't say 'The Sandy.' I said, 'This is Andy.' I wanted to know what I had to bring for science tomorrow, only that tomorrow was last year and I got in trouble because you never called back."

"That was you? Why was your voice so gravelly?"

"I had a cold. You knew I had a cold."

"Let's not argue," Rachel said. "We've got to clean."

And they did. Rachel and Tamika wiped the table and swept the floor. Andy stood by the sink, but he wasn't in the mood to wash dishes. *It seems I'm never in a dishwashing mood,* he thought.

When Rachel and Tamika weren't looking, he put the dirty dishes in the cabinet. He piled a few clean plates on top of the dirty ones so no one, especially Aunt Janet, would notice. He swept everything from the floors under the living room rug. Yesterday's newspaper was on the coffee table, so Andy hid it under one of the couch pillows. While Rachel checked the bedrooms and Tamika put things away in the front hall, Andy checked the bathrooms.

The toilets were flushed. The toothpaste was put away. The towels were straight. *Something is missing,* Andy thought. *Signs! Aunt Janet likes signs.* He hurried to his room and made signs. Then, just as he finished taping them to the bathroom walls, the doorbell rang.

Andy, Rachel, and Tamika hurried to the front

door. Rachel peeked through the peephole. "It's Aunt Janet," Rachel whispered. "Are we ready?"

"No," Andy said. "Tell her we're not home. Tell her we moved. Tell her anything. Just don't open the door."

The doorbell rang again.

Rachel opened the door.

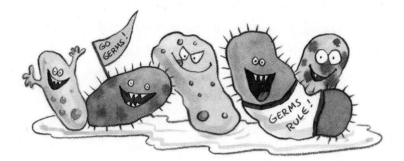

Chapter 3
Smile! We're Watching You

Aunt Janet stood in the doorway. Beside her was a large shopping bag with bottles of cleaning liquid, a mop, and a broom. She was looking at her watch.

"What time is it?" she asked.

"Three forty-seven," Rachel answered.

"Are you sure?" Aunt Janet asked. "Then why does my watch say four fifty-three?"

"I bet she blames us for that, too," Andy mumbled.

"What? What did you say?"

Tamika spoke loud and clear. "You live in a different time zone. You must have forgotten to set your watch back when you came here."

"And maybe it's running six minutes fast," Andy offered.

"Running fast," Aunt Janet said as she reset her watch. "It shouldn't be running fast."

"Complain, complain," Andy whispered. "That's all you do."

"What? What did you say?"

"I'll take your things," Andy said real loud.

He grabbed the bag. The mop handle hit his head as he hurried to follow Aunt Janet into the house. The broom fell out of the bag.

"Here, I'll take it," Aunt Janet said as she picked up the broom and put it back in the bag. "You're not very good with mops and brooms."

And you're not very good with nine-year-old boys who try to help, Andy thought.

Rachel closed the door.

Aunt Janet looked directly at Tamika and said, "So you're Tamika Anderson. I'm really happy to meet you. I'm going to make dinner, and everyone says I'm a creative cook. You'll see."

Then she turned to Andy and said, "And I'm so happy to see you."

Aunt Janet leaned close to Andy. "Oh my, your face is dirty. There are germs in dirt. Lots of germs. You should clean your face. It's important to be clean."

"So bossy," Andy mumbled as he went to the bathroom to wash his face.

"That's why I'm here, to get the house clean for the baby. Did you know," Aunt Janet asked Tamika, "I'm a nurse?"

"Yes," Tamika said. "Andy and Rachel told me."

"Well, I'm not *really* a nurse. I'm a nurse's aide. And I do lots of cleaning."

"There," Andy said. "My face is washed."

"Good. Good," Aunt Janet said. "You know, when your face is dirty, you're wearing germs. Now, let's go to the kitchen. When a kitchen is dirty, you're eating germs."

Aunt Janet followed the children into the kitchen.

"We already cleaned here," Rachel said proudly. "And we cleaned upstairs, too."

Aunt Janet opened the cabinet, lifted the top plates, and took out one Andy had put away. Maple syrup was stuck to it. "There are germs on these plates, sticky germs."

How did she do that? Andy wondered. *How did she know I hid dirty plates under the clean ones?*

Rachel looked at the plate. Then she glared at Andy and said, "*He* should clean them."

"No, I'll mop," Andy said. "That should be fun."

"Yes," Aunt Janet agreed. "Andy can sweep and mop. He needs practice doing that. He should learn how to handle mops and brooms. Rachel, please do the dishes. Tamika and I will go upstairs. We'll clean the bedrooms and bathrooms."

"Don't clean the bathrooms," Andy said. "They're already clean."

"Oh, no. The bathrooms may *look* clean but that's where germs hide," Aunt Janet said. "But they can't hide from me. And I want Tamika to help me, so I can get to know her."

Aunt Janet took two bottles of cleaning liquid from her bag and went upstairs with Tamika.

Andy put up his hands and told Rachel, "Sorry. I should have washed the dishes better. But I didn't think anyone would notice."

He took the mop.

20

"Didn't you think we'd notice when we took out the dishes and set the table?" Rachel asked.

Andy hadn't thought of that.

"And why didn't you want Aunt Janet to clean the bathrooms? Did you hide dirty plates there, too?"

"No," Andy answered. "I cleaned there and I did a good job."

All of a sudden, he dropped the mop. "Oh no! But I put up signs. I thought they were funny, but now I don't think Aunt Janet will like them."

"What signs?"

Andy started to sweep. "I put a NO SWIMMING sign over the toilet," he said.

Rachel laughed.

"LIFEGUARD ON DUTY," Andy continued. "I put that sign over the bathtub. And a SMILE! WE'RE WATCHING YOU ON HIDDEN CAMERAS sign on the mirror."

"Just wait until Aunt Janet sees them," Rachel said. She laughed. "Hey, I'm not mad anymore about the dirty plates. You'll get in enough trouble for the signs."

Andy swept the kitchen floor. He was about to sweep the dirt into the pantry and close the door, but stopped. *She'll know,* Andy thought as he took out the dustpan. *Aunt Janet has radar— dirt radar.*

Andy wanted to do a good job of mopping the floor. He made the mop real wet and mopped from the door, around Rachel's feet, under the table, and to the other end of the kitchen. There were just two dry spots left, one around Rachel and one around Andy.

"Now look at what you did!" Rachel hollered. "You've mopped me into a corner. If I walk across the floor, my shoes will make dirty prints. And if I take off my shoes, my socks will get wet. Now I have to wait here for the floor to dry."

"I'm stuck, too," Andy said. "I'm not making dirty prints with Aunt Janet around."

He stood there, surrounded by wet floor, and watched Rachel clean the dishes.

"We finished the bedrooms," Aunt Janet announced as she walked into the kitchen. "We'll clean the bathrooms later." She stopped, looked at the very wet floor and then at Andy. He was still holding the mop. "What happened here?" she asked him. "Why is the floor so wet?"

"I cleaned it," Andy answered proudly.

"Oh," Aunt Janet said. "And you kept squeezing

the dirty water out of the mop. Right? Of course that's right. You didn't mop the floor with dirty water."

"I didn't?" Andy asked.

But, of course, he did.

I used plenty of water but that's not good enough for Aunt Janet, Andy thought.

"Well, I can't wait for the floor to dry," Aunt Janet said. "It's time to prepare dinner."

She walked quickly into the kitchen and slipped on the wet floor. She grabbed the refrigerator door handle as she fell, but the door opened and Aunt Janet landed on her bottom! Tamika, Andy, and Rachel rushed over and helped her up.

Andy quickly covered his mouth. He was about to laugh. Rachel looked at Andy. She was about to laugh, too.

"Oh, please, get me a chair. I have to sit."

Rachel brought her a chair.

The seat of Aunt Janet's skirt was wet. She sighed when she sat down. Then she yelped, "That hurts!"

What hurts? Andy wondered. Then he remembered what she landed on when she fell and he knew what hurt.

Aunt Janet squirmed until she was comfortable.

Rachel put her head down and continued to wash the dishes. She didn't want to look at Aunt Janet. She knew if she did she would begin to laugh.

"First I put away dishes without washing them and that was wrong," Andy mumbled. "Then I wash the floor and that's wrong, too. The water was dirty and too wet. Now it's my fault that water is wet! Everything is *my* fault!"

"What?" Aunt Janet asked. "I can't hear you when you mumble."

Andy didn't answer.

Aunt Janet groaned as she tried to get up. Her eyebrows went up and her lips curled down into her beagle look. She sat down again.

"I'll need help preparing dinner," she said. "Please, move the table here. I'll make your dinner sitting down."

Andy and Tamika moved the kitchen table.

"Now, please, open the refrigerator and tell me what's inside."

Tamika opened the refrigerator.

Andy looked inside.

"Milk," he called out, "and leftover spaghetti with tomato sauce."

"I'll fry it with bread crumbs," Aunt Janet said. "Do you have bread crumbs?"

"No," Andy answered. "All our bread is the big kind."

"Oh, that's too bad. What else is in the refrigerator?"

"Orange juice, carrots, leftover chicken soup, margarine, yogurt, cottage cheese, eggs."

"Eggs. Good." Aunt Janet nodded. "Do you have any canned or frozen vegetables?"

Tamika opened the pantry. "We have cans of corn, string beans, peas, lima beans, and that's it."

"I just had an idea. I know what I'll make," Aunt Janet said. "Please, get me a mixing bowl, a large spoon, eggs, milk, string beans, and peas."

What in the world is she cooking? Andy wondered.

"I'm making you a special treat."

Rachel brought her the mixing bowl. Andy brought her the milk and eggs. Tamika opened the cans of peas and string beans and brought them to Aunt Janet.

26

Aunt Janet cracked the eggs and put them in the bowl. She added the milk and vegetables.

"What are you doing?" Andy asked. "Eggs, string beans, and peas don't belong together."

"I'm fixing dinner," Aunt Janet told him. "I'm making a string bean and pea omelette."

Andy imagined eggs with green things stuck inside.

"I don't think this is right," he told Aunt Janet. "When the hen laid those eggs, she didn't want them cooked with string beans and peas."

Aunt Janet looked blankly at Andy.

Andy spread out his arms—he was about to make an important statement. "A string bean pea omelette is a betrayal of Mrs. Hen," he said. "I'm sure she had dreams for her little eggs and there were no string beans and peas in those dreams."

"I think you're right that hens dream," Aunt Janet said. "You could prove it by studying their eyes. You could watch them when they sleep and see if their eyeballs move. But I don't think you could find out what they dream about."

Aunt Janet used the large spoon to mix the eggs and vegetables.

"I don't know if hens dream about omelettes," she said. "But sometimes *I* do. You know, I dream of creating the perfect omelette, something different, and winning a cooking contest."

Just then the telephone rang.

Rachel picked up the phone.

"It's Dad!" Rachel squealed. "It's Dad!"

Chapter 4
The Animals Must Go

"What's he saying?" Andy asked Rachel. "Do I have a brother?"

"*Shhh!*" Rachel told Andy. "I can't hear Dad."

"Tell Dad I want to talk."

Rachel listened for a moment. Then she asked, "What's taking so long?"

Rachel listened some more.

"Really! She said that?" Then Rachel added, "OK, Dad. Good-bye," and she hung up the telephone.

"Hey," Andy protested. "I wanted to talk."

"Dad had to go to Mom," Rachel said. "The baby isn't born yet. And Mom asked the same thing I did. She said, 'What's taking so long?'"

"Babies are worth the wait," Aunt Janet said dreamily. "Babies are so cute."

"They are?' Andy asked. "Was I cute?"

"Oh yes," Aunt Janet said. "You were so cute."

She stretched her arms out to show Andy just how cute he was. She was still holding the large spoon. Raw egg, string beans, and peas dripped onto the floor.

Aunt Janet looked down. "Oh my," she said. "This floor is a mess."

"I just cleaned it," Andy said.

Yuck! Andy thought. *I said, "I just cleaned it." That's something Aunt Janet would say. What's happening to me!*

Aunt Janet put the spoon on the table, smiled, and asked, "Have you ever seen a newborn baby?"

"I have," Rachel answered. "I saw Andy."

Tamika said, "I've seen lots of babies. Sometimes, when I went to visit my parents in the hospital, I saw people leaving with babies that were just a few days old."

Tamika's parents were injured in a car accident and while they were in the hospital, she needed a place to stay. First she stayed with the Russells' neighbors, the Perlmans. Then the Perlmans had to go to South America for a research project. That's when Tamika moved in with the Russells.

Tamika's parents were doing better. They had left the hospital and moved to a rehabilitation center. Tamika hoped she and her parents could go home soon.

"I've seen lots of newborns," Andy said proudly. "My gerbils have babies all the time—and not just one. They have lots."

"Do you still have gerbils in the house?" Aunt Janet asked.

"I have other animals, too," Andy told her. "I love animals."

"I had a dog once, a collie," Aunt Janet said. "But my landlord made me give it away. He said it was too big to keep in my small apartment."

"Well, my gerbils are small and this house is big, so I'm not giving them away."

"I named him Sparky," Aunt Janet said, "and wow, did he make a mess. My apartment always looked dirty."

"Gerbils don't make a mess," Andy said.

"He's right," Rachel said. "He keeps all his pets in the basement, and he keeps them in tanks, so there's no mess."

"Slither is not messy and Sylvia is *really* not messy," Andy added. "She's my goldfish and lives in water. It's like she's taking a bath over and over again."

Aunt Janet said, "Sparky loved it when I gave him a bath. I was so sorry I had to give him away."

"Well, I'm not giving my pets away!" Andy said and ran out of the kitchen.

Tamika followed him out. "What's wrong?" she asked.

"Aunt Janet wants me to give away my pets."

"She didn't say that."

"Oh, you don't know her. She's not your aunt. She's strange. She dreams about omelettes."

Tamika shook her head. "Maybe she *is* strange, but right now you're the one who's acting strange. She was just talking about her dog."

"She said she had to get rid of Sparky because he was messy," Andy said. "Why do you think she said that? She was telling me I'll have to get rid of my pets, too, because they're dirty. That's exactly what she was saying and I won't do it!"

Chapter 5
Friends for Dinner

"W here did you two go?" Aunt Janet asked when Andy and Tamika returned to the kitchen.

"Nowhere," Andy answered.

"Oh," Aunt Janet said and continued to mix the eggs, string beans, and peas. "Well, I'm glad you're back."

She looked at her watch. "Oh my," she said. "Look at the time! I have to finish getting dinner ready."

Aunt Janet stirred the eggs some more. When she lifted the spoon, the egg mixture dripped from the spoon into the bowl.

Yuck! Andy thought. *That looks terrible.*

"Please, help me up," she said. "My whatchamacallit still hurts and I've got to get to the stove to make your dinner."

Tamika took one of Aunt Janet's arms. Rachel took the other. They helped her walk to the stove. Then Rachel gave Aunt Janet the margarine and a frying pan.

Andy watched Aunt Janet pour the mixture of eggs, string beans, and peas into the frying pan. *What sort of a person,* Andy wondered, *wants to chase lovable animals from their homes?* Aunt Janet stirred the eggs with the spoon. *And what sort of person does such horrible things to food?*

"You know what we should do?" Tamika said. "We should make signs to welcome the baby."

"Signs!" Rachel protested. "That's silly. Babies can't read."

"Well, I think it's a good idea," Aunt Janet said as she fried the eggs. "I love signs. We can put pictures of them in the baby's album. Later, when we take them down, we can put the signs in the album, too."

Oh my gosh, Andy thought. *Signs! I don't want Aunt Janet to see my bathroom signs. I want her in a good mood, in a sure-you-can-keep-your-pets mood.*

"I've got to go to the bathroom," Andy announced and started out of the kitchen.

"Hurry," Aunt Janet told him. "Dinner is almost ready."

Andy stood right outside the kitchen door. *I've got to get rid of those signs,* he thought, then started up the stairs. *But I'd better do something to protect the gerbils, Slither, and Sylvia from Aunt Janet. That's more important. I have to save my animals.*

He hurried back down the stairs and started toward the basement.

"There you are," Aunt Janet called out. "Dinner is ready."

Dinner is ready! Who wants to eat eggs and string beans? Not me! And how am I going to save Slither and the gerbils? Andy slowly entered the kitchen. He needed a plan.

He thought about all his gerbils. He had about twenty. *I'll glue feathers on them. I'll break open a pillow, take out the feathers, and glue them onto Slither and the gerbils. I'll tell Aunt Janet they're birds. Everyone likes birds.*

Andy shook his head. No, that was no good. The glue would hurt the gerbils, and birds weren't long and thin like his snake, Slither.

I could make the tanks look like television sets, with oaktag and construction paper. I could tell Aunt Janet the sets are on and tuned to an animal program.

Andy shook his head again. *What am I thinking! This isn't a TV cartoon. It's real life. And even if she did think it was a TV, she might try to change the channel,* Andy thought. *Then she'd know.*

"Why are you shaking your head?" Aunt Janet asked. "Why aren't you eating?"

Andy looked at Aunt Janet. Then he looked at the yellow and green eggs on the table. *That looks terrible. I bet it tastes terrible, too.*

"Please, sit and eat," Aunt Janet said.

Andy shook his head. He wasn't going to eat.

"I think I'll enter these in a cooking contest. I'll call them Janet's Vege-Eggs," Aunt Janet said. "You should taste them, Andy."

"I don't want to," Andy answered.

"Why not?"

"You dream of omelettes and I don't. You think scrambled eggs should have green things in them and I don't. We're different people," Andy told Aunt Janet.

"Oh my," Aunt Janet said. "Of course we're different, but that's no reason not to eat eggs."

"They're not so bad," Rachel said. She ate a forkful of green egg to prove it.

Traitor, Andy thought.

"Of course they're not bad," Aunt Janet said. "They're very good."

"It's not the eggs," Andy declared. "I won't eat something made by someone who is chasing my friends from their home."

"What friends?" Aunt Janet asked. "I wasn't chasing any friends. Tell them to come have dinner with us."

"Really?" Andy asked. "Okay, I'll tell them to come up."

Andy hurried out of the kitchen and down to the basement. He looked at Slither. "You're so cute," he said, "but I'm not taking you up to meet Aunt

Janet. Some people don't like snakes. I'm taking one of the gerbils."

Andy looked in the three gerbil tanks. He wanted to pick the cutest one to show Aunt Janet.

She won't want to get rid of my pets, Andy thought, *if she sees how cute they are.*

Andy watched the gerbils run through the tunnels and on the exercise wheel. He looked into one of the tanks, and at first he couldn't decide which one to bring upstairs. They all looked cute to Andy. Then one gerbil stopped playing and looked right back at Andy. Andy wrinkled his nose and the gerbil did, too.

"You're cute," Andy told the gerbil.

The gerbil had light brown fur and a long tail. It seemed to be smiling at Andy.

"You're the one!" Andy told the gerbil. "You're the one I'll show Aunt Janet."

Andy took the gerbil from the tank. He closed the screen on top of the tank and checked to make sure it was completely closed. He didn't want any gerbils to get loose while Aunt Janet was in the house.

"Keep smiling. Be cute and charming," Andy

instructed the gerbil as he went up the basement steps. "I want Aunt Janet to like you."

Andy stopped at the entrance to the kitchen.

"She'll ask you to try her Vege-Eggs, but you don't have to," Andy told the gerbil. "Just be cute."

Then he walked in.

Chapter 6
Look at the Sweet Animal

Aunt Janet looked up. She saw Andy walking to the table. Then she saw the gerbil.

"A mouse!" she screamed. "Oh my goodness! What's a mouse doing in the kitchen?"

"It's a gerbil," Andy said as he walked closer, "and it's perfectly harmless."

"It has germs. All animals have germs. That's why we never allow them in the hospital."

Andy spoke in what he hoped was a soothing

tone. "This gerbil is my friend and it doesn't have germs."

Andy was standing close to the kitchen table, but Aunt Janet had moved her chair. She was almost against the wall.

"Get it away!" Aunt Janet shouted.

"You said to bring my friends to dinner. Well, this is my friend."

"Please, your gerbil looks just like a mouse and I'm afraid of mice. Ask your dad. I've always been afraid of mice."

Andy looked at the gerbil. He couldn't understand why Aunt Janet didn't think it was cute. And he didn't understand how anyone could be afraid of anything so small. He was sure once she saw it she would let him keep the gerbils in the house.

Andy looked back up at Aunt Janet. She had her hands up, in front of her face. Her eyes were open wide.

"Please, get it away," Aunt Janet pleaded.

Andy stepped back.

"Animals carry germs and disease," she repeated.

"Germs!" Andy cried. "Diseases! My animals are healthy."

"I clean and scrub to keep my patients and their hospital rooms clean."

"My friends are clean," Andy said.

"I gave Sparky lots of baths, sometimes three a day," Aunt Janet said, "but I never brought Sparky to the hospital."

Andy looked past Aunt Janet at Rachel and Tamika. "Did you ever hear Slither, Sylvia, or one of the gerbils cough or sneeze?" he asked them.

Both girls shook their heads.

"You see?" Andy said in triumph. "They're not germy."

"Please, put the animal back in its cage. Then come back and wash your hands with soap and water."

Andy whispered in the gerbil's ear, "I'm taking you back to your friends."

"What did you say?" Aunt Janet asked. "You know I can't hear you when you mumble."

"I said I'm going."

She told me to invite my friends. Well, she didn't mean it! Andy thought as he left the kitchen. *She just wants them out.*

When Andy reached the basement door, he stopped. He took a deep breath and whispered to the gerbil, "Don't you worry. No one is getting rid of you."

Andy walked down the basement steps. He put the gerbil in its tank. Then he looked at Slither, Sylvia, and the three tanks filled with gerbils. He really meant what he said, that Aunt Janet would not get rid of them.

Andy stood there for a moment and thought. He was only nine years old. Aunt Janet was an adult. He knew he couldn't really *stop* Aunt Janet from doing anything. *But if I can't stop her, how will I keep her from getting rid of my pets. How?*

Andy looked in the gerbil tank again. He saw some of the gerbils. Others were hidden in the tunnels.

Then Andy smiled. He knew just what he would do.

Chapter 7
Eggs, String Beans,
Peas, and Soap

I'll hide you," Andy told the gerbils. "If she can't find you, she can't get rid of you. Even Aunt Janet can't do that."

The gerbils weren't listening. They were running through tunnels, eating from their food bowls, and drinking from their water tubes.

"Now the big question is, where can I hide all of you?"

Hmmm, Andy thought and looked around the basement. *We have all these board games. I'll take out the boards and cards and phony money and put all that stuff in the snake and gerbil tanks. Then I'll poke holes in the boxes so the animals can breathe.*

But that was no good. It would be too dark inside and he couldn't be sure the boxes would stay closed. The animals could get out.

Andy opened the cellar door and looked in there. *I could hide them behind the clothing boxes,* he thought, *but it's so dark. And if Aunt Janet can find a few dirty plates, she can definitely find a snake, a goldfish, and twenty gerbils.*

Andy returned to the basement and looked at the three gerbil tanks and Slither's tank. *Why does the good news of having a baby have to be ruined by bad news?* he wondered. *Why are such big people afraid of such little animals?*

"Andy," Rachel called. She was standing at the top of the basement stairs. "You should come up. Aunt Janet is waiting for you to eat the eggs."

"She is?"

Rachel nodded.

"She wants you to taste them, to see if you like them," Rachel explained, "or if you think she should add orange slices and cranberries to the recipe."

"Oranges, cranberries, string beans, peas, and eggs," Andy said. "She hates gerbils and loves strange food. Some aunt!"

"And Andy," Rachel added, "why did you bring the gerbil into the kitchen?"

"It's my friend."

"I know. I like the gerbils, too, but Aunt Janet doesn't," Rachel sighed.

When Andy and Rachel walked in through the kitchen door Aunt Janet said, "Please, wash your hands and try my Vege-Eggs."

Andy walked to the sink. He turned the faucet and put his hands under the water.

"Use soap," Aunt Janet told him. "In the hospital we always wash our hands with soap. It's a rule."

Andy squirted liquid dishwashing soap onto his hands. He rubbed his hands together until there was lots of lather. He spread the lather up to his elbow. Then he washed it off and started again. This time he put the stopper in the sink.

The sink quickly filled with water. Andy covered his hands and arms with soap and dipped them in. Water from the faucet hit his arms and spilled onto the floor.

"SHUT THE WATER OFF!" Aunt Janet and Rachel shouted.

Andy turned the faucet. He took out the stopper and watched the water go down the drain. Then he dried his hands, went to the table, and sat down. Aunt Janet loaded a plate with eggs, put it in front of Andy, and said, "You'll like it. You really will."

Andy stuck his fork into the eggs. He poked around, looking for some egg without string beans or peas.

"It's one of my best dishes," Aunt Janet said.

Andy put a little on his fork and tasted it.

"Yuck!" Andy mumbled.

"What? What did you say?" Aunt Janet asked. "Did you say 'Yum?' It *is* good, isn't it?"

Andy looked at his plate. There was so much Vege-Egg on it. He *couldn't* eat it all.

He pushed his fork in and brought up some more egg. This time there was a string bean in the egg. He nibbled it.

Yuck! Andy thought, but he didn't say it this time. *It tastes like you used soap, too, like you cooked with soap.*

"Eat it quickly," Tamika whispered. "Before your taste buds taste it."

"Tasty? Did you say it's tasty?" Aunt Janet asked Tamika. "Do you want more?"

"No! No, thank you," Tamika quickly replied.

Aunt Janet looked at Rachel.

Rachel shook her head, patted her stomach, and declared, "I'm full."

"Well," Aunt Janet said to Andy. "That leaves plenty for you."

She smiled at him and asked, "Do you have the sign upstairs because of the gerbils?"

"What sign?"

"The NO SWIMMING sign in the bathroom. Is it for the gerbils, to tell them not to swim in the toilets?" She smiled. "You know, gerbils can't read."

Oh no! Andy thought. *She saw the signs!*

"Um," he stammered. "It's not for anyone. The sign is a joke."

"I know," Aunt Janet said. "And when I asked if they were for the gerbils, I was joking, too."

"You were joking?"

Aunt Janet smiled.

Maybe that's what these are, Andy thought. *Maybe these eggs are a joke.*

"Go on," Aunt Janet said. "Eat your dinner."

Andy nibbled a little more egg. He knew he should do what Tamika said, eat it real quickly, so the taste torture would be over, but he just couldn't do it.

Aunt Janet watched Andy nibble. She smiled.

Andy wanted to scream, to tell her the Vege-Eggs tasted terrible, but he didn't. He nibbled some more egg. And while he ate he thought about his pets.

Hey, she doesn't want my pets in this *house. That's the answer. I'll just take them to another house. I'll take them to the Perlmans'.*

Dr. and Mrs. Perlman lived next door to the Russells. Andy knew he could get into the Perlmans' house because Tamika had a key. Mrs. Perlman had asked her to watch the house.

I'll bring all the tanks to the Perlmans' and when Aunt Janet leaves, I'll bring them back.

Andy was happy. Now he just had to find a way to sneak his snake and gerbils and goldfish out of the house so they would be safe.

He nibbled some more egg. *Yuck!* He thought again. He had found a way to save his animals, but it seemed nothing would save him from Aunt Janet's egg disaster.

He nibbled some peas.

RRRRing!

It was the telephone. Rachel hurried from her seat to the counter to grab it. Tamika and Aunt Janet turned.

I'm saved! Andy thought. While Aunt Janet was looking at Rachel, he quickly took a handful of egg, put it in his pants pocket, then wiped his hand on the back of his shirt.

"It's Dad!" Rachel said.

She listened for a moment. Then she screamed, "YES!"

Chapter 8
What's Up?

Mom had the baby," Rachel announced. "It's a boy!"

"Hooray!" Andy and Tamika screamed.

"That's wonderful," Aunt Janet said. "Please, let me speak to him."

Rachel gave her the telephone.

Aunt Janet asked Mr. Russell lots of questions about the baby, how much he weighed, how long he was, and if he was healthy. She also asked about Andy's mom.

"Yes, yes," she said. "I made them dinner. I created something new: Vege-Eggs."

She looked at Andy's plate.

"The children ate it all, even Andy," Aunt Janet said proudly.

Rachel and Tamika looked at Andy's plate, too. They were surprised to see it was empty.

"Can I talk to Dad?" Andy asked.

Aunt Janet gave Andy the telephone.

"Hey, Dad, how's the baby?"

"Your little brother is so cute," Mr. Russell said. "He looks just like you did when you were a baby."

"What color hair does he have? Is he a righty or a lefty?"

"Righty or lefty! What kind of question is that?" Rachel laughed. She grabbed the telephone. "What do you think the baby is doing now, writing a letter?"

"When can we see Mom and the baby?" Rachel asked. She listened for a moment and then told the others, "We can visit tonight, at eight."

Tamika spoke to Mr. Russell next. Then she gave the telephone to Aunt Janet.

"Congratulations again. We'll see you very soon," she said and hung up the telephone.

"That's wonderful news!" Aunt Janet exclaimed. "Now we have to hurry. We have to get ourselves ready to visit the hospital. And we have to get the house ready for the baby."

"Are you still hungry?" she asked Andy. "Do you want more Vege-Eggs?"

"No!" Andy said. "I mean, no, thank you."

"Then let's clean up. Someone has to scrub the frying pan and wash the dishes. And one of you has to sweep."

Andy began to clear the table.

"Why don't you make the signs," Aunt Janet said to Andy. "It would be nice if we had them up when your mother and brother come home."

"Yes. The signs," Andy said.

This is my chance to rescue my pets, he thought.

"I'll make them on the computer. It's in the basement."

Andy hurried downstairs.

"The signs will have to wait," Andy told Slither, Sylvia, and the gerbils. "I've come to rescue you. I'm taking you to the Perlmans'."

Andy reached around one of the gerbil tanks. He carefully took it off the shelf. It was big and heavy. As soon as the tank moved, the gerbils went wild.

"Don't be scared," Andy told them.

But they *were* scared.

Andy couldn't see where he was going so he took one small step at a time. He walked toward the stairs. He felt the first step with his foot. He slowly walked up.

"I've got to put you down," he told the gerbils. "I've got to see if Aunt Janet is still in the kitchen."

Andy put the tank on the floor, right outside the basement door. He quietly walked toward the kitchen. He heard Aunt Janet's voice and could see her back. She was standing by the stove. Andy opened the front door just a little and hurried back to the gerbils.

"She's busy," he told them. "Now's our chance."

Andy picked up the tank and quietly carried it to the front door. He used his foot and opened it wide enough to get out. He carried the tank across his front yard and onto the Perlmans' porch. He put the tank down and turned the doorknob. It was locked, of course.

"I forgot to get the key from Tamika," Andy told

the gerbils. "Don't worry. I'll be right back and I'll bring your friends."

Andy hurried home. He went to the kitchen. Tamika was washing dishes and Rachel was drying them. He didn't see Aunt Janet.

"Tamika," Andy whispered, "I have to talk to you."

Tamika put the dish she was washing back in the sink. She followed Andy out of the kitchen.

"What's up?" Tamika asked.

"Where's Aunt Janet?"

"She's sitting down," Tamika said. "She still hurts from her fall."

"She blames me for that, I bet. She's always blaming me for something."

Tamika shook her head. "She didn't say it was your fault. She just said it hurt."

Andy told Tamika about his plan to hide Slither and the gerbils. He asked her for the key to the Perlmans' house.

"I think you're making a mistake," Tamika said. "Aunt Janet never said you have to give away your pets. She said *she* had to give away her dog."

"Didn't she say animals aren't allowed in a hospital?"

61

Tamika nodded.

"And didn't she say this house has to be as clean as a hospital?"

Tamika nodded again.

"You see," Andy said. "I'm one step ahead of her. I'm a whole staircase ahead of her. There's one thing I know and that is you have to keep ahead of Aunt Janet. Now, will you please help me save my pets?"

"OK."

Tamika went upstairs. When she came down she gave Andy the key to the Perlmans' house. She asked him if he needed help carrying the animals next door.

"What I really need is for you to keep Aunt Janet in the kitchen looking the other way, away from the front door."

"I can do that," Tamika said.

Tamika went back to the kitchen and Andy went to the basement. He took the second gerbil tank and quietly carried it out of the house.

"You'll be visiting the Perlmans for a while," he told the gerbils. "They're not home, but you would like them. They're nice."

Andy put this tank next to the other one. He unlocked the front door and went inside. At first he thought he would put the animals on the kitchen table. But then he remembered what Aunt Janet said about gerbils and food and thought Mrs. Perlman might not like having them in the kitchen. She might not like it if he put them in the living or dining rooms, either. He decided to put them in Dr. Perlman's office. That was Andy's favorite room. He loved the old brass and wood barber's chair, the mechanical bank, and the menorah with all the flowers.

Andy put the tanks on Dr. Perlman's desk.

"I'll visit you every day," Andy told the gerbils. "I'll bring you food and water."

Then he hurried home. He opened the door... and there was Aunt Janet.

"Did you hang the signs outside?" she asked.

"Not yet," Andy answered. "I didn't finish making them. I'll do that now."

"Good," Aunt Janet said. Then she turned and went upstairs.

Andy hurried to the edge of the stairs and watched Aunt Janet go into the bathroom.

63

Chapter 9
I Know! The Garage!

Andy went downstairs.

"Evan was born," he told Sylvia the gold-fish, "and Dad said he's cute, just like I was as a baby." Then he turned to Slither and the remaining gerbils and said, "I'll get you to the Perlmans', just as soon as I make a few signs for my brother."

Andy sat at the computer. He typed WELCOME! and added a picture of two babies, a boy and a girl, in diapers. He set the computer to print four copies of the sign.

Evan, Andy thought. *He'll be just like me and love animals.*

He got up and reached around the last gerbil tank. "We're going to the Perlmans'," he informed the gerbils and took the tank off the shelf. "But as soon as Aunt Janet is gone, you'll come back and you'll get to meet Evan."

Andy slowly walked up the basement steps. When he got to the top, he listened. He didn't hear anyone nearby. He started toward the front door and then he saw her. Aunt Janet was standing with her back to Andy and looking out the long, narrow window in the door.

I've got to get out of here, Andy thought. *And fast!*

Andy turned. Then, in his hurry to get downstairs, his legs got tangled. He fell. He landed first on his knees, then on his elbows. The tank fell from his hands and landed on its side. Luckily, it didn't break, but the screen on top came off. Andy quickly got up. He grabbed the screen and held it in place before any of the frightened gerbils could get out.

Aunt Janet ran to Andy. "What happened?" she asked.

"I saved the gerbils," Andy told her.

"Oh my, are you hurt?" Aunt Janet put on her worried beagle face.

"No, they don't hurt me. They don't bite and they don't have germs."

"But I thought they were already down-stairs . . . Oh, just hurry," Aunt Janet said. "We're going to the hospital soon."

Andy picked up the tank. "Don't worry," he whispered. "I'll save you." Then he told Aunt Janet, "I'm taking them to the basement."

"Hurry," Aunt Janet repeated. "We're going to the hospital soon."

Andy opened the basement door and waited. When Aunt Janet was in the kitchen, he turned and started toward the front door.

"Let's go," Aunt Janet called.

She was walking toward the front door.

"I can't take you to the Perlmans'," Andy told the gerbils. "She'll see us. I have to take you some-where else."

Andy looked around. Then he saw the door to

66

the garage. He leaned the tank against the door. He reached under the tank and opened the door.

The garage was filled with boxes, old furniture, and toys. Andy put the tank on the old kitchen table. He didn't like seeing his friends with all the family junk, but he was glad Aunt Janet wouldn't know where they were.

"You can't trust her," Andy told them. "She thinks you're mice and she hates mice."

"Andrew," Aunt Janet called. "We're ready to go."

I'll have to save Slither and Sylvia later.

Andy waited. He didn't want Aunt Janet to see him coming out of the garage. He didn't want her to know where he hid the gerbils.

He heard Aunt Janet start her car.

Honk! Honk!

"Bye," he told the gerbils.

Andy rushed from the garage and out of the house.

"Wait for me!" Andy shouted. "Wait for me!"

Chapter 10
Look at Him

Andy ran to the front of the house. He started to open the back door of the car, where Rachel and Tamika were sitting. It was a small car, but Andy would rather sit crowded in the back with them than up front with Aunt Janet.

"Please, get in front with me," Aunt Janet said.

Andy opened the front door on the passenger's side. He looked back at Rachel and Tamika.

They knew Andy did not want to sit with Aunt

Janet. Rachel struggled. She tried not to laugh. But she did.

"Is something wrong back there?" Aunt Janet asked.

Rachel held her hand over her mouth.

"No," Tamika said and giggled. "Nothing is wrong."

Andy put on the seat belt and looked straight ahead. Aunt Janet backed the car out of the driveway. She drove down the block and turned onto the main road. She was driving *so* slowly.

Can't you go a little faster? Andy thought. *I want to see Evan.*

Aunt Janet drove past a sign: SPEED LIMIT 35 MILES PER HOUR. Andy looked at the speedometer. The needle pointed to exactly thirty-five.

Wow, Andy thought. *Aunt Janet really follows rules.*

Andy imagined her in school, in fourth grade like him.

If the teacher said, "No talking," Aunt Janet would never talk, even when she got home. Poor little Janet Russell. When she came home her mom would say, "Tell me, how was your day?" But little Janet Russell wouldn't answer.

Andy wondered what *little* Aunt Janet looked like and what she liked to do. *I bet at recess she liked to play with buckets, mops, and brooms.*

The traffic light turned yellow and Aunt Janet stopped the car.

"When we get to the hospital, take a look at how clean it is," Aunt Janet said. "That's part of my job, keeping the hospital where I work clean. Clean is important."

Here it comes, Andy thought. *She's going to say that animals aren't clean.*

But Aunt Janet didn't say that. The traffic light changed to green and she slowly drove away from the light. When they reached the end of the next block, Andy looked at the speedometer. The needle pointed again to exactly thirty-five.

Aunt Janet turned into the hospital parking lot.

"We're a few minutes early," she said after she parked the car. "That will give us time to buy something in the gift shop."

Andy, Rachel, and Tamika followed Aunt Janet into the hospital. Mr. Russell was in the lobby waiting for them. He hugged them all.

"You should see Evan," he said. "He's so cute. He's got Rachel's eyes and nose and Andy's ears."

71

"Doesn't he have anything of his own?" Andy asked.

Mr. Russell laughed and said, "Sure he does. He has a little dimple in his chin. Neither of you have that."

Andy looked at Rachel. *Her nose and eyes! My ears! That doesn't sound cute. Maybe it's the dimple,* Andy thought. *Maybe that's what makes Evan so cute.*

"Just wait till you see him," Mr. Russell said.

Mr. Russell took them to the desk. "They don't let children upstairs, just brothers and sisters," he whispered. Then he told the woman that Andy was the baby's brother and Rachel was the baby's sister. "And," he said, "Tamika is like a member of our family. She's almost Evan's second sister."

The woman smiled and said they could all go up.

"But I wanted to buy a toy for the baby," Aunt Janet said.

"Evan doesn't need new toys. He can play with Rachel and Andy's old things."

"Really?" Andy asked.

"Sure," his father told him as they walked to the elevator. "He's your brother."

"Are the toys clean?" Aunt Janet asked. "If Evan is going to play with them, they have to be clean."

Here it comes, Andy thought again. *You were just waiting to tell Dad that toys have to be clean and, of course, that I can't have germy animals in the house.*

But Aunt Janet didn't say that.

The elevator door opened. The Russells, Tamika, and an old lady with a cane got on.

Mr. Russell pressed the button for the fifth floor. The woman pressed the button for the third floor.

The woman spread her feet slightly apart. She held her cane with both hands and leaned slightly forward.

"We had a baby," Andy told her.

The woman smiled.

"His name is Evan and my dad built a new room in our house," he went on. "It was the attic. In a few months the baby will move into my room and I'll move upstairs."

The woman smiled.

"I helped build it."

The elevator door opened. It was the third floor.

73

The woman still had both hands on her cane. She didn't move to get off the elevator.

Mr. Russell held the doors open and told the woman, "I think this is your floor."

The woman smiled.

Mr. Russell pointed to the large *3* on the wall just outside the elevator.

"Oh my," the woman said as she got off. "Thank you."

When the door closed, Mr. Russell smiled and told Andy, "I don't think she heard you. She didn't hear me, either."

The elevator door opened again. It was the fifth floor. Everyone followed Mr. Russell through two large doors, past a long desk, to a hall lined with windows. On the other side of the windows were lots of bassinets. There was a baby in each one. And there were lots of people in the hall looking through the windows at the babies.

Mr. Russell went to one of the middle windows. "There he is," he said and pointed. "Evan is right there."

Andy looked at his baby brother. He was sleeping. Evan looked so small to Andy, even for a baby. Then Andy looked at the babies in the other

bassinets. They looked small, too, just as small as Evan.

Andy stood there and watched his brother. Evan wasn't doing very much, just lying there and sleeping, but still, Andy was fascinated. *He really is cute,* he thought.

The baby girl in the bassinet next to Evan's woke up. She started to cry.

"*Shhh.* Quiet," Andy whispered. "Don't wake my brother."

But she did wake him. Evan opened his eyes. He stretched his little arms and legs, opened his mouth, and started to cry.

Look at him, Andy thought. *He's even cute when he cries.*

Andy looked up at his father and Aunt Janet. They were both smiling. Andy saw tears in Aunt Janet's eyes.

I wonder if she was standing here and smiling nine years ago. Maybe there were tears in her eyes then, too, when she saw me for the first time. Maybe she really did think I was cute.

"Let's go," Mr. Russell whispered. "Let's visit Mom."

Mr. Russell walked past the windows to the

doors at the other end of the hall. Rachel, Tamika, and Aunt Janet followed him. Andy was reluctant to leave his brother, but he didn't want to be left there alone, and he did want to see his mother. He hurried and caught up with the others.

They all followed Mr. Russell to room 518. There were two beds in the room. Mrs. Russell was in the first bed. Another woman was in the second bed, the one near the window. Mrs. Russell was resting.

"Shhh," Mr. Russell cautioned. "We don't want to wake Mom."

"I'm awake," Mrs. Russell said and opened her eyes. "Did you see him? Did you see our Evan?"

"Yes," Aunt Janet said. "He's beautiful."

Rachel, Tamika, Mr. Russell, and Aunt Janet all talked at once. They talked about how beautiful the baby was, about his sweet round face, his light blonde hair, and the little dimple in his chin.

Andy just listened.

"What about you?" Mrs. Russell asked Andy. "What do you think?"

"I think he's perfect," Andy said.

Mr. and Mrs. Russell smiled. Then Aunt Janet

looked at her watch. "It's late," she said. "Visiting hours are almost over. We should go."

"Yes," Mrs. Russell agreed. "And I need to rest. Soon, Evan and I will be home, maybe tomorrow. Then there'll be plenty to do."

Great, Andy thought. *Then Aunt Janet will leave.*

Andy, Rachel, and Tamika kissed Mrs. Russell.

"Thank you, Janet," Mrs. Russell said, "for taking care of the children."

"If you want," Aunt Janet offered, "I can stay for a few days to help, so you can rest."

NO! Andy thought.

But Mrs. Russell said, "Oh yes. That would be great."

Chapter 11
Worse than Vege-Eggs

W e can't go yet," Rachel said once they were
out of Mrs. Russell's room. "We have to say
good-bye to Evan."

They went to the nursery. Evan was sleeping.
His small hand with its five tiny fingers was outside the blanket. Andy looked at his own, much
bigger, hand. He couldn't imagine that his hand
was once as small as Evan's.

"Visiting hours are over," Aunt Janet said. "We
have to go."

"Bye, brother," Andy said quietly. "I'll see you tomorrow."

In the car, Aunt Janet said, "Right now he just drinks milk. But when he gets older, I'll make baby food for Evan."

Andy said, "I don't think you should make him Vege-Eggs."

Aunt Janet laughed. "Of course not. I'll make creamed carrots and spinach and chicken."

Yuck! Andy thought. *That sounds* worse *than Vege-Eggs.*

"When we get home," Aunt Janet said, "We have to finish cleaning the house. We have to make it hospital clean. And Andy, you have to put up your WELCOME, EVAN signs."

"Welcome, Evan," Andy said. "Welcome, Evan. That gives me a great idea for a sign. I'll write WELCOME TO EVANSVILLE. His name is Evan and Evansville is a real place."

Aunt Janet stopped at a traffic light and told the children, "I'm going to do the laundry tonight, so give me what you're wearing when we get home and get in your pajamas."

Pajamas! Andy thought. *First I have to rescue*

the gerbils from the garage and take them to the Perlmans'. I have to take Slither to the Perlmans', too.

Aunt Janet parked the car in the driveway. When she opened the door to the house she reminded the children, "Finish your jobs and get into pajamas. In twenty minutes I'll start the laundry."

Only twenty minutes! Andy thought. *I have to work real fast.*

He hurried downstairs. He turned the computer on.

"Let's go," he urged the computer. "Let's go."

The motor hummed. The screen lit up. Information about the computer's memory and antivirus program flashed on the screen. Andy wasn't interested in any of that. He was in a rush.

Finally he could begin. He typed WELCOME TO EVANSVILLE in the sign-making program. Then he set the file to print.

The printer made its getting-ready noises and Andy took Slither's tank off the shelf.

"We're going for a little trip," Andy told Slither. "We're going to the Perlmans'." Then, as he

carried the tank upstairs, he whispered, "We have to be very quiet."

Andy opened the basement door and listened. He heard the water in the kitchen sink running. He heard someone walking about upstairs. Andy walked slowly toward the front door.

"What's that?" Aunt Janet asked. She was standing at the top of the stairs.

Andy turned. He had hoped to get safely outside before Aunt Janet could see the tank and Slither.

"Is that your goldfish?" Aunt Janet asked as she walked down the stairs. "I like goldfish."

"It's Slither," Andy said quickly and went out the front door.

Andy rushed over to the Perlmans'. He left Slither there. Then he rescued the gerbils from the garage and took them to the Perlmans', too. He decided Sylvia would be safe at home, since Aunt Janet liked goldfish.

Andy looked at the four tanks on Dr. Perlman's desk. He was glad they were safe, but he worried about what would happen next. He wondered what his dad would say when Aunt Janet told him that animals have germs.

Tonight, when Dad gets home, I've got to talk to him first, Andy thought, *before Aunt Janet gets to him. Once she talks to him about germs and babies, it will be too late.*

Chapter 12
What Did I Do Now?

Andy said good-bye to his animals and went home. He hoped he could hang up his signs without seeing Aunt Janet. Then he would change into his pajamas and wait in bed by the window and watch for his dad.

Andy opened the front door and looked into the kitchen. Rachel and Tamika were there, but not Aunt Janet. He looked upstairs. He didn't see her there, either. Andy went to the basement and there she was. She had a bucket of ammonia-smelling water and was washing the floor.

"What are you doing?" Andy asked. "That stuff smells terrible."

"I'm cleaning with ammonia. It's what we use in the hospital," she said. "It kills germs. I'm starting down here and I'll work my way up."

Andy was glad his animals were at the Perlmans'. He didn't think they'd like the ammonia smell.

Aunt Janet pointed to the fish tank and asked, "Is that Slither?"

"No, that's Sylvia."

"Why don't you keep Slither and Sylvia together?" Aunt Janet asked. "Goldfish are a lot like people, you know. They like company."

Andy was glad Aunt Janet thought Slither was a fish. She was afraid of gerbils, so he was sure she'd be afraid of a snake.

"I took Slither to a neighbor's house," Andy said.

Aunt Janet washed the counters and the computer stand.

Andy took the WELCOME TO EVANSVILLE sign and the others from the printer. He shut off the computer and went upstairs. He was glad to get away from Aunt Janet and the ammonia.

Andy hung all four signs in the hall, one on top of the other, opposite the front door. He stood back and admired his tower of signs:

WELCOME!

WELCOME!

WELCOME!

WELCOME TO EVANSVILLE!

Evan is going to love this, he thought.

"It looks good," a voice said.

"Is that you, Evan? Do you really like it?" Andy asked.

"No, it's us," Rachel and Tamika said, giggling. They were on the stairs.

"Oh. Oops." Andy went upstairs to change. He had just taken out his pajamas when he heard a scream from the kitchen. He rushed downstairs.

Rachel and Tamika were standing in the kitchen, right by the answering machine.

"Listen to this!" Tamika said. "My mother called while we were at the hospital."

She pressed the PLAY button.

Message one.

"Good news, Tamika. No, it's great news! I'm coming home tomorrow. That's right! Dad needs to stay here a while longer, but I'm coming home. And, since *I'm* coming home, so will you. I'm so happy! Hey, where are you? Well, I'm calling Aunt Mandy now. I hope she'll pick me up and take me to the Russells'. Then we'll go home together. I can't wait to see you."

Andy looked at Tamika. He had seen her smile before, but not like this. Her smile seemed to stretch from one ear to the other.

Tamika picked up the phone to call her mother but the line was busy. "I'll wait a few minutes and try again," she told Andy and Rachel. Then she played the rest of the messages.

Message two.

"Hello, Mr. and Mrs. Russell, this is Tamika's aunt Mandy. I'll come by tomorrow afternoon, after school, with Tamika's mom. Then we'll take Tamika home! Thank you for being such good friends to her. I'll see you all tomorrow. Good-bye."

"I'm so happy for you," Rachel said.

"I think I'm happy, too," Andy added. "No. I *know* I'm happy for you, but I'm sad for me. I really liked having you here."

89

"But I'm going home," Tamika said. "I'll miss you, too, but I'm going home."

Message three.

"Carol? Carol? Are you there? This is Jake. Please, pick up."

"There's no Carol here," Andy, Rachel, and Tamika said and laughed. "Poor Jake."

Jake waited. "Please," he pleaded again. "Did you forget my number? Here it is." And Jake left his telephone number.

That was your last message.

"I want to listen to Mom's message again," Tamika said and pushed the *Save* button.

"And I want to call Jake."

Andy dialed Jake's number.

"Hello, Jake," Andy said. "You keep dialing the wrong number and asking for Carol."

"I do?"

"Yes. And that's why Carol doesn't call back."

Andy told Jake the telephone number he was calling.

"Oh no! I switched the 2 and the 3 and then kept pressing *Redial*. Thank you so much."

Andy sat on one of the kitchen chairs and smiled.

I bet Carol has been waiting for Jake's call, he thought.

Tamika and Rachel were still standing by the answering machine.

Tamika listened to her mother's message again and Andy thought about the first time he met her. He was in the second grade. Tamika and her parents had just moved into a house nearby and Tamika transferred to Andy's school. Andy was struggling with reading and Tamika helped him.

A year later, in third grade, Mr. Harris, the principal, came into class with the horrible news about her parents' car accident.

Andy remembered the many things they had done together, especially the visit to Aunt Mandy's. *As soon as we walked up to her building,* Andy remembered, *a hamster fell out of the sky. And it had a parachute!*

Andy really liked having his best friend living in his house. They had so much fun together. She even helped him study. Andy often forgot to bring a book or an assignment home, but Tamika never forgot things in school.

Andy went upstairs. *Things are happening so*

fast, he thought as he got out of his clothes and threw them in the hamper. *Mom and Evan are coming home tomorrow and Tamika is leaving.* Andy sat on his bed, by the window, and watched for his dad.

He heard Aunt Janet go to the hamper and take the clothes out. He was glad his door was closed. Whenever she saw him, it meant trouble.

Andy looked at the clock by his bed. It was already past ten. He was tired, but determined to stay up and speak to his father about his pets before Aunt Janet did.

He looked at his book bag. He hadn't done his homework. He hoped his dad would write a note to his teacher, Ms. Roman. She couldn't expect someone who just had a baby brother to do his homework, could she?

Andy put his pillow against the wall. He stretched out on his bed with his head on the pillow and looked out the window. It was dark outside and boring.

This is like watching a television that's not turned on, Andy thought.

He was falling asleep.

"Andrew!"

Andy sat up.

"ANDREW!"

It was Aunt Janet.

What did I do now? Andy wondered.

Chapter 13
Egg, String Beans, Peas, and Lint

A ndy hurried off his bed and downstairs. Aunt Janet was in the laundry room. She held up Andy's pants and asked, "Are these yours?"

"Yes. I wore them today."

Aunt Janet walked into the kitchen. She put the pants on the table and said, "Please, reach in this pocket."

Oh no! Andy thought. He remembered what he had put in there.

"Go on. Put your hand in."

Andy slowly put his hand in his pants pocket. "What's in there?"

"Egg."

"It's the Vege-Eggs I made for dinner, isn't it?"

That's one of those rhetorical questions, Andy thought, *the kind you don't answer.* So he didn't answer it.

"You should have told me you didn't like them and I would have made you something else."

Sure, Andy thought. *Fish-Eggs, or Liver-Eggs, or Broccoli-Eggs.*

Aunt Janet said, "It's not that you didn't like my dinner that bothers me so much. It's that you were afraid to tell me. I'm your aunt."

"But you think everything I do is wrong," Andy protested. "You're always angry at me."

"I don't know what you're talking about," Aunt Janet said. "I really don't. I haven't been angry at you."

Andy just stood there. He didn't know what to say.

"I'm not even angry now."

"You're not?"

"You know," Aunt Janet said, "you wouldn't be the first one to tell me you didn't like something I made. I once made eggplant-chicken pancakes for your dad. I served them with maple syrup. They were delicious, but your dad didn't like them. He tasted the pancakes and then ate a bowl of cereal."

"Were you angry with him?"

"No. And I'm not angry with you."

RRRRing!

Andy picked up the telephone receiver.

"Hello."

"Hello. This is Jake. You called me a while ago. You told me I dialed the wrong number and thanks to you I dialed the *right* number and spoke to Carol. And you know what?"

"What?" Andy asked.

"She was waiting for my call. She's not angry with me."

"I'm glad," Andy said.

Carol was not angry with Jake, and Aunt Janet was not angry with him!

Andy heard a key go into the front door lock. He quickly said good-bye to Jake and hurried to greet his father.

Rachel and Tamika ran downstairs and Tamika told Mr. Russell about her mother's call.

"Mom and I are going home," Tamika announced.

"That's great," Mr. Russell said and hugged Tamika. "We'll miss you, but still, we're so happy for you, Tamika."

Then they all walked into the kitchen.

"So many good things have happened today," Mr. Russell said. "Evan was born. Mom feels fine. And now Tamika's mom is going home from the rehabilitation center."

"How are you?" Aunt Janet asked Andy's father. "Are you hungry?"

"I'm so happy," Mr. Russell said, "and yes, I'm hungry, too."

"Hey, look what's on the table," Rachel said and laughed. "You could eat what's coming out of Andy's pants pocket."

Mr. Russell turned and looked at the pants that were still on the table.

"Eggs! Vegetables! How did eggs and vegetables get into your pockets?"

"Well . . . ," Andy began.

"It was my fault," Aunt Janet said. "I didn't ask the children what they wanted to eat. I just decided. And Andy was too polite, too nice, to tell me he didn't like what I made."

"I was?" Andy said. "I was too nice?"

"Yes," Aunt Janet said and smiled. "You were."

Andy smiled and thought, *So many good things did happen today. Evan was born. Tamika found out she will be going home. And Aunt Janet thinks I'm nice.*

"I'll make you something," Aunt Janet said to Mr. Russell. "What would you like?"

Mr. Russell shook Andy's pants. Some Vege-Eggs fell onto the table.

"What is this? What did you make?" he asked Aunt Janet.

"I told you about it when we spoke. It's eggs, string beans, and peas. It's Vege-Eggs."

Aunt Janet wiped the eggs off the table. She shook Andy's pocket out over the sink. Then she took his pants into the laundry room.

"Now," she said, returning to Mr. Russell. "What should I make for you?"

"Well," Mr. Russell replied, "I don't want Vege-Eggs and I don't want eggplant-chicken pancakes. I think I'll just have cereal."

"Oh, cereal again," Aunt Janet said.

Andy smiled.

Aunt Janet looked at Andy.

"You didn't have any supper. Would you like some cereal, too?"

Andy nodded.

While Andy and his father ate, Andy talked about his pets.

"Can I keep them?" he asked his father. "They don't have germs and they won't get loose."

"Of course you can keep them."

"I like the fish," Aunt Janet said, "but not the gerbil."

"Andy doesn't have one gerbil," Mr. Russell explained. "He has about twenty of them."

Aunt Janet held her hand to her heart. "Twenty!" she cried and sat down. "That's a lot."

"They're not here," Andy said. "They're visiting the Perlmans."

"But the Perlmans are in South America!" Mr. Russell said.

Andy told his father and Aunt Janet all about Slither, the gerbils, and the Perlmans. He said he would bring them back to the basement.

"And I know what *I'll* do," Aunt Janet said.

"What?" Andy asked. "You can't do anything to my pets. My dad said I could keep them."

"Why would I do anything to your pets? I'll just stay out of the basement," she said, smiling.

Chapter 14
Who's Talking about
High School?

Bam! Bam!
        Andy opened his eyes.
Bam! Bam!

He sat up in bed and looked outside. It was still dark. He looked at the clock beside his bed. It was six o'clock.

Bam! Bam!

The noise was coming from Rachel's room. Andy got out of bed and knocked on Rachel's door.

"Hey! What's going on in there?"

"I'm helping Tamika get her things together," Rachel told Andy as she opened the door. "She wants to be ready when her mom and Aunt Mandy come."

Tamika's suitcase was open on the floor. It was filled with her clothes. There was a pile of books on Rachel's bed. Tamika was standing by the bookcase. She took a book out and asked Rachel, "Is this mine?"

Rachel looked at it and replied, "Yes, that's yours."

Tamika threw the book. *Bam!* It hit the wall beside Rachel's bed and dropped onto the pile.

"*That's* what woke me up," Andy said.

"Do you want to help?" Tamika asked.

"Sure."

Andy brought some shopping bags from the kitchen. He put Tamika's books, radio, and other things in the bags. Then, while Andy and Rachel got ready for school, Tamika called her aunt Mandy.

"She says they'll be here when we get home from school," Tamika told Andy and Rachel at breakfast.

Andy filled his bowl with cereal.

"I'm too excited to eat!" Tamika said.

Andy was excited, too, but not too excited to eat. He had two full bowls of cereal.

"It's time to catch the bus," Mr. Russell called. "And when you get home, Mom and Evan will be here."

"And my mom and Aunt Mandy," Tamika added.

"Yes, *everyone* will be here," Mr. Russell said.

Andy was the last one out of the house. When he got to the bus stop, Tamika had already told the Belmont sisters she was going home. And Rachel had told them about Evan.

"It's great news about you going home," the bigger Belmont said. "But I'm not so sure about having another Russell boy on the block."

"Very funny," Andy said.

The school bus stopped and the door opened. The Belmonts got on first, followed by Rachel, Tamika, and Andy.

Rachel and Tamika told Mr. Cole, the bus driver, their news.

Andy sat next to his friend Bruce.

Rachel, Tamika, and the Belmont girls sat down

and Mr. Cole got up. He held up both his hands and the children in the bus stopped talking.

"I have two happy announcements," he said. Then he told everyone the good news. Mr. Cole started to clap. Soon everyone was clapping.

"When I visit," Bruce said, "we can all play together."

Andy told Bruce, "He's a baby. We won't be able to play with him for a long time. But we can start reading to him and telling him things now."

When they arrived at school Mr. Cole told Andy, "I'll bet you'll have lots of trouble paying attention in class today. You'll be thinking about the baby."

"Yeah," Andy said. "I'm sure I will."

I always have trouble paying attention.

Mr. Harris, the principal, was standing in the front hall of the school.

"Congratulations," he told Andy. "I guess, pretty soon, your brother will be coming to this school."

"I don't think so," Andy said. "I think Evan will stay home for a few years."

Mr. Harris smiled.

"Congratulations," Andy's teacher, Ms. Roman,

said as he walked into class. "And I'm really happy for you, too," she said to Tamika.

"Hey," Andy asked. "How does everyone know about the baby and Tamika's mom?"

"This morning your father called. He told us you both didn't have a chance to do your homework last night. He also said you might be a little distracted today."

That means I don't have to pay attention, Andy thought. *Good old Dad.*

Andy sat in his seat, just behind Stacy Ann Jackson. She congratulated Andy, too.

Andy copied the homework assignment from the chalkboard. Ms. Roman gave a geography lesson about rivers and lakes. Andy listened to the beginning of the lesson. Then he remembered what Ms. Roman had said, that she knew he might be distracted.

She knows I might not be able to pay attention, so why should I?

He looked at Tamika. Her notebook was open and she was listening to the lesson.

What a waste, Andy thought. *Why is she listening when Ms. Roman said she doesn't have to?*

Andy knew that right now Evan was a baby, but still, he closed his eyes and dreamed about playing with him when he was older, showing him how much fun it is to watch the gerbils run through their tunnels, and teaching him to love animals. Andy dreamed through the geography, science, and math lessons. He dreamed until Stacy Ann told him it was time for lunch.

Andy sat in the lunchroom with Tamika, Bruce, and Stacy Ann.

"Are you hungry now?" he asked Tamika.

"No, not really," she said. "I'm still real excited."

Tamika opened the lunch bag Aunt Janet had packed for her.

"But I'll eat," she said.

Andy opened his lunch bag. He wondered what Aunt Janet gave him. He reached in and took out a note. *Your dad said you like cream cheese sandwiches, pretzels, and apple juice. I hope he's right. If not, you can buy something else.*

A dollar was taped to the note. The note and dollar were from Aunt Janet. Tamika had a note and dollar, too.

While they ate, Andy talked about Evan, and

Tamika talked about her parents. Then, with Aunt Janet's two dollars, they bought cake and shared it with Bruce and Stacy Ann.

In the afternoon, while the others in the class were reading, Andy looked at Tamika and thought about not having her in the house anymore. It almost seemed like he was trading Evan for Tamika.

When the school day ended, and Andy was leaving, Ms. Roman said to him, "I'm sure you're very excited about your brother. You probably didn't get much sleep last night. Well, you have the whole weekend to rest up. When you come back on Monday, I expect you to pay attention."

"You do?"

"Yes," Ms. Roman said and smiled. "I do."

On the bus ride home, Andy sat next to Bruce.

"Yesterday," Bruce said, "I was about to go out for the bus and Mom stopped me. 'Are you going out like that?' she said. I didn't know why she said that until I looked down. I had on my shirt, socks, and sneakers, but I was still wearing my pajama bottoms. 'When are you going to grow up?' she asked me."

"Really?" Andy asked.

But right then, Andy wasn't interested in Bruce's problems. He was thinking about Evan.

"When will I?" Bruce asked. "When will I grow up?"

"I don't know," Andy answered. "I think it all happens slowly, a little at a time."

Someone should tell that to Mr. Harris, Andy thought. *Evan won't be here soon. By the time he's in this school, I'll be in high school.*

"Don't worry," he told Bruce. "It's a long time before we'll be in high school."

"High school! Who's talking about high school?"

Just then the bus stopped at Bruce's block. "Bye," he said and hurried off.

Everyone is in a hurry to grow up, Andy thought. *But I'm not. I'm happy being nine.*

Andy got off at the next stop. He saw his parents' car in the driveway. That meant they were home from the hospital with Evan. There were two other cars in front of the house, Aunt Janet's and Aunt Mandy's.

Andy, Rachel, and Tamika crossed the street. The front door was open. Aunt Janet and Aunt Mandy were standing outside. Tamika's mom was just inside. She was in a wheelchair.

109

"Mom!" Tamika shouted and ran to her.

Tamika and her mother hugged. There were tears in their eyes. Aunt Mandy stood beside them and smiled.

Rachel and Andy were anxious to see Evan. They said hello to Tamika's mom and aunt and then rushed upstairs. Then, halfway up the stairs, Andy stopped. "Mrs. Anderson," he called out, "I'm glad you're better."

"Thank you, Andy. I am, too," Tamika's mother said. "Now, go up and see your brother. He's adorable."

Andy ran up the rest of the stairs.

There was a crib next to Mrs. Russell's bed. Evan would sleep in his parents' room for a few months. Then he would move into Andy's room and Andy would move upstairs.

Andy's mom waved to him. She wanted them to come in.

They quietly walked into the room and looked in the crib. Evan was sleeping.

"Isn't he sweet," Mrs. Russell whispered.

Evan did look sweet.

Andy looked at his brother, his tiny hands and fingers, his cute nose, and the dimple in his chin.

111

He walked away from the crib and whispered to his mother, "He's so small."

"Yes, he is," Mrs. Russell said and smiled. "But soon he'll be big, as big as you."

Soon! It won't be soon, Andy thought. *It will be a long time before Evan is as big as me.*

Aunt Janet walked by. She was carrying a laundry basket full of clean clothes to Rachel's room.

Tamika came upstairs. "I'm going now," she whispered.

Mrs. Russell kissed her and said, "Come back and visit."

Tamika hugged and kissed Mrs. Russell. "Thank you for being so nice to me," she said.

Andy and Rachel helped Tamika carry her things to Aunt Mandy's car. Andy and Aunt Mandy pushed Mrs. Anderson's wheelchair outside and helped her into the car.

"Thank you," Mrs. Anderson said and kissed Andy's cheek. "I thanked your parents a few times for helping us, but I didn't thank them enough. Please, tell them again how grateful I am."

When she was ready to leave, Tamika looked

at Andy and Rachel and said, "This is the hardest part, saying good-bye to you."

Andy bit his lower lip. He didn't want to cry.

"You don't have to say good-bye to us," Rachel said. "We'll see you in school."

"That's right," Andy said.

Then he remembered what his father had told the woman at the hospital. "And even if you're not living here," Andy added, "you're still like a member of our family."

It was difficult for Andy to see Tamika ride off, but she was going home.

When Andy came into the house he realized that in the past two days, so much had changed. Tamika had gone home. He had saved his pets from Aunt Janet when he really didn't have to. And he had become an older brother.

Andy was glad he was growing up—he just didn't want to grow up too fast. Being nine was just fine. Right then, Andy thought it was the very best age of all.

Read the other books in the Andy Russell series to see how all of Andy's troubles began!

The Many Troubles of Andy Russell

Escaped gerbils, wrong answers in school, and a tough situation with his best friend—Andy's got all sorts of problems! And things won't be settling down anytime soon, thanks to a *big* secret his mother reveals.

> "It won't be long before [Andy Russell] next hits hot water. Readers will likely be standing by when he does."—*Publishers Weekly*

Andy and Tamika

Things just keep going wrong for poor Andy Russell. How could those gerbils have escaped *again*? And how can he pay attention at school with a new baby brother or sister on the way? Maybe his best friend, Tamika, can help him stay out of trouble.

> "The various plot lines provide plenty of humor and action, which is enhanced by Will Hillenbrand's lively drawings."—*Booklist*

School Trouble for Andy Russell

Substitute teachers can mean only one thing . . . BIG trouble. When his classmates' tricks land Andy in the principal's office, he's got to prove his innocence before it's too late!

> "Filled with fun and misadventure. Poor Andy!"—*School Library Journal*

Parachuting Hamsters and Andy Russell

An exciting weekend in the big city with Tamika and her aunt doesn't go quite as Andy expected. Who wants to go to stuffy restaurants, art museums, and the ballet? And who is dropping hamsters off the top of Aunt Mandy's building? Andy is determined to find out!

> "Thoroughly engaging."—*School Library Journal*

Andy Russell, NOT Wanted by the Police

Something is going on at the Perlmans' empty house next door. Now it's up to Detective Andy Russell to prove to his family—and to the police—that he's not making it all up (*really!*).

> "[This mystery] will have young readers flying through it to find out exactly what is going on next door."—*Kirkus Reviews*